For Laura, who is such a brilliant mom ~ S.S.

For Mom, Dad, Becky, Joe,
and S-J with all my love always ~ K.H.

tiger tales
5 River Road, Suite 128, Wilton, CT 06897
Published in the United States 2019
Originally published in Great Britain 2018
by Liontree Publishing Ltd.
Text copyright © 2018 Stephanie Stansbie
Illustrations copyright © 2018 Katy Halford
ISBN-13: 978-1-68010-154-6
ISBN-10: 1-68010-154-4
Printed in China
LTP123HS0919
10 9 8 7 6 5 4 3

For more insight and activities, visit us at www.tigertalesbooks.com

My FRiENDS AND ME

by STEPHANiE STANSBiE

Illustrated by KATY HALFORD

tiger tales®

Do you know my friend **Kate**? She has **two** dads.

Kate's
_daddy

Frank
_

Kate's dads are pretty cool.

They take her out for brunch.

(In case you're wondering, that's breakfast and lunch all at once.)

My **best** friend, Harry, has one mom. And she's the **greatest**!

Harry's mom is **mega** good at . . .

baking **cakes**,

skills

YUMMM

cool moves

sword fights,

Bon-Bon the bear

and super **soft** cuddles.

awww!

My friend Olivia has two sisters, two moms,
and one little brother named Bean.

Olivia

Olivia's mama

face plant!

That's a whole **volleyball** team!

My other friend Lily
is **seriously** lucky.

She has **two** houses,

two

wardrobes,

Maggie

Max

two

beds,

and

two

bathtubs!

Mabel

Lily **always** beats her dad at cards.

(She almost never cheats.)

And her mom lets her stay up really, **really** late!

My three favorite **sleepover** friends are . . .
Jade (who has a **huge** house),

real-life butler!

Johnny (with his cozy camper),

and Jasper (who lives on an actual boat!).

My friend Hannah has a foster mom.

She smells like candy and

is absolutely **fantastic** at juggling.

My friend Ned lives with his sister

and two hamsters.

She takes him surfing all the time.

That's pretty awesome—for a grown-up!

But the **coolest** grown-ups
I know are my **grandma**
and **grandpa**.

You won't **believe**
the things we do!

What I like the **most** is when we're back at home,
snuggled up and planning our next big **party**.

Roly

Ralph

The thing with grown-ups is,

it doesn't matter who they are or where they live—

they're fantastic at loving us . . .